A BLUE TALE

and Other Stories

FOREWORD BY *JOSYANE SAVIGNEAU*

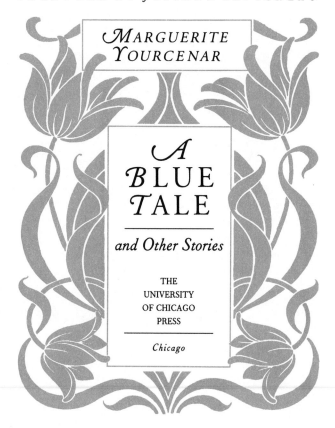

MARGUERITE
YOURCENAR

A
BLUE
TALE

and Other Stories

THE
UNIVERSITY
OF CHICAGO
PRESS

Chicago

TRANSLATED BY *ALBERTO MANGUEL*

TEXAS WOMAN'S UNIVERSITY LIBRARY

The University of Chicago Press, Chicago 60637

The University of Chicago Press, Ltd., London

© 1995 by The University of Chicago

All rights reserved. Published 1995

Printed in the United States of America

04 03 01 00 99 98 97 96 95   1 2 3 4 5

ISBN: 0-226-96530-9 (cloth)

Originally published in Paris as *Conte bleu; Le Premier soir; Maléfice,*
© Éditions Gallimard, 1993

Photograph of Marguerite Yourcenar on p. vii courtesy the
Petite Plaisance Trust.

Library of Congress Cataloging-in-Publication Data

Yourcenar, Marguerite.

    [Short stories. English. Selections]

    A blue tale and other stories / Marguerite Yourcenar ; foreword by
Josyane Savigneau ; translated by Alberto Manguel.

    p.   cm.

    Contents: A blue tale—The first evening—An evil spell.

    1. Yourcenar, Marguerite—Translations into English.   I. Manguel,
Alberto.   II. Title.

PQ2649.O8A25   1995

843'.912—dc20

    95-14507
CIP

♾ The paper used in this publication meets the minimum requirements of the
American National Standard for Information Sciences—Permanence of Paper
for Printed Library Materials, ANSI Z39.48-1984.

CONTENTS

Marguerite Yourcenar
Circa 1929

F O R E W O R D

TO LOVE A WRITER is to wish the writing might never cease. That is why, after the writer's death and before resigning ourselves to rereading only, we comb through the files and stray papers in the hope, so often unfulfilled, of discovering an unpublished masterpiece, an astounding private journal, a shattering exchange of letters. Having exhausted all these avenues, there remain what lovers of literature call "curiosities" or "documents"—quickly branded by their denigrators as "scrapings from the bottom of the barrel." True, there is no clear line between the two; it depends on our fondness for the writer in question, and also on our desire to understand as fully as possible the writer's progress—that is to say, the life.

When Marguerite Yourcenar died in December 1987, she left behind an unfinished manuscript, the first part of her family trilogy *Quoi? L'Eternité*, published in 1988; a collection of essays that she had prepared for publication (*En pèlerin et en étranger*,

1989); several fragments of what would have been
her final thoughts on one of her passions, travel (*Le
Tour de la prison*, 1991); and, finally, a number of letters that must still be sorted out, selected, and anno-
tated before being published. These are the most
important texts. There are others—"curiosities"—
three of which make up the present little volume:
"Conte bleu" ("A Blue Tale"), "Le premier soir"
("The First Evening"), and "Maléfice" ("An Evil
Spell"). As often happens with great writers, these
three brief stories share a coherence that might not
have been suspected when it was decided to bring
them together.

All three were written between 1927 and 1930.
In 1927, Marguerite Yourcenar was twenty-four
years old. In 1930, she had just published her first
novel—actually a novella, *Alexis ou le Traité du vain
combat*, 1929 (translated as *Alexis*), and the decade
which she later referred to as her "settling-in
period" was coming to an end; she called these texts
"the projects of my twentieth year." In 1924, at the
age of twenty-one, she began working on the book
that was to become *Mémoires d'Hadrien (Memoirs of
Hadrian)*, and by 1929 she had drafted several ver-

sions of the novel, in whole or in part, one of them in dialogue form. In 1926, she offered one of these versions to the publisher Fasquelle, under the title *Antinoos;* it was turned down. Also during this period she began sketching the character of Zeno, another essential figure in Yourcenar's oeuvre. And "A Blue Tale" was in the same vein as *Nouvelles Orientales (Oriental Tales)*, or, at least, it was a first step in that direction.

However, it would be wrong to surmise that by 1930 everything had been "played out" for Yourcenar, that her literary goals had been achieved. And yet her fate had certainly been sealed by the fact that she had become conscious of it. Everything she said about the projects of her twentieth year, everything that can be gleaned from a meticulous chronological reading, reveals her very particular approach, the manner in which she conceived the writing of her books: developing, refining, strengthening, composing, and rethinking throughout an entire lifetime that which she had imagined or dreamed up between the ages of eighteen and twenty-eight. By the end of the decade she was convinced she had become a writer. Later, during an interview, she would recall

the joy with which, in November 1929, she held in
her hands the proofs of her first book. "I said to my-
self: Well! There are at least a few hundred, maybe a
thousand French writers that one can more or less recall. At last, here I am, feeling that I belong among
them, that I am somewhere in that crowd." She had
no doubt that the future would prove her right. This
was a useful certainty with which to resist all those
who, throughout the years, would try to tell her, as
they do with every writer, that she had not really
written anything of value.

To one who loves Marguerite Yourcenar, these
declarations of self-confidence are exhilarating. All
the paths that have led to great books should be ex-
plored; so we are almost as eager to read, examine,
and analyze the "minor texts" as those great books.

Of the three stories in this collection, only "A
Blue Tale" was previously unpublished. "The First
Evening" appeared in December 1929 in the *Revue
de France* (9th year, volume 6, no. 23) under the
name "Marg. Yourcenar." "An Evil Spell," signed
"Marguerite Yourcenar," was published in the 829th
issue (44th year) of the *Mercure de France* in January
1933. By then the author had been critically recog-

nized, notably by Edmond Jaloux, for her first novel, *Alexis*, published in November 1929. The publisher Grasset, through the recommendation of André Fraigneau, had published another novel, *La Nouvelle Eurydice*, in 1931 as well as an essay on Pindar in 1932 (the first book in which the author's first name, "Marguerite," appears in full on the cover, rather than the indeterminate "Marg.").

Why was "A Blue Tale" never offered to a magazine? Perhaps because it was the first section of a never-completed triptych. The typescript of "A Blue Tale" was filed away, with several others, in Yourcenar's office at Petite Plaisance, her house in the United States, in North East Harbor, Maine. At the top of the first page were several notes in Yourcenar's hand: "written about 1930" (when she had begun the stories later collected in *Oriental Tales;* "Kali décapitée" ["Kali Beheaded"] appeared in the fourth issue of the *Revue européenne,* April 1928); "the idea was also to write a 'Red Tale' and a 'White Tale'"; "Keep—maybe this text could appear in a volume along with 'Sixtine' and a few others. [signed] M. Yourcenar (May 1950)." "Sixtine" was published in 1983 in the collection *Le Temps, ce*

grand sculpteur (That Mighty Sculptor, Time). "A
Blue Tale" was not among them. Was Marguerite
Yourcenar still planning to some day write the
"White Tale" and the "Red Tale" mentioned in her
note of 1950? In her case, without knowing that she
herself said so, it is difficult to say she was not, since
her conviction of carrying out all the projects she had
once outlined was strong to the point of obsession.
In any event, only "A Blue Tale" has reached us.

It is a very short story, cleverly crafted to give
the impression of imitating an ancient oral tradition.
It is a tale with few surprises, since it concerns itself
strictly with a few simple themes: the desire for
riches; men's credulity when lured by money; the
difficult attainment of the object supposed to make
one rich (in this case, sapphires). Its structure fol-
lows all the obligatory stages of dispossession: acci-
dents, shipwrecks, pirate attacks, deaths, wanderings,
poverty even greater than before the acquisition of
the supposed fortune, final destitution. To these are
added the rituals peculiar to Yourcenar, such as self-
mutilation. It is the atmosphere of the story rather
than the plot that foreshadows *Oriental Tales*. And
the writing, in spite of certain fumblings (one might

have dispensed with the eyes that "had befriended the darkness"), bears characteristics of the style that Yourcenar was to develop in the late 1930s: uttermost attention to every sensation, and the desire to express each one as faithfully as possible. Furthermore, "A Blue Tale" owes its title not merely to the sapphire cavern, the easternmost destination of the European merchants who are the story's heroes, but to Yourcenar's decision to describe reality in tones of blue. What could be merely a device, a young writer's experiment, becomes a fully successful venture, which is why this story is no doubt the most satisfying of the three texts. Yourcenar's Oriental inspiration is here in full swing. The characters that would concern her throughout her life (beginning with Hadrian, that most Greek of all Roman emperors) all long for the Orient, in the broadest sense of the word. In this story, the only merchant to be saved is, of course, the Greek, the most detached from material riches, willing to forgo the sapphires and return to his fishing; after the shipwreck he will be led back to Tinos by a dolphin. The others, through an excess of greed, will either die or be condemned to poverty.

"The First Evening," which in its own dry manner does not lack stylistic qualities or a sense of narrative, is of greater biographical interest. It can be considered the final stage in the game played between Yourcenar's father and his daughter, since it is a text written by the former and revised and published by the latter. We know how much both loved this ambiguity, the mysterious pleasure of substitution that signaled a rare intimacy and a reciprocal fascination. Michel de Crayencour wasn't afraid of undertaking, in his daughter's name, the necessary negotiations with a publishing company in order to have Marguerite's early efforts published. After his exchange of letters with one publisher—several of which are in longhand and therefore easily identifiable—*Le Jardin des chimères* appeared under Perrin's imprint in 1921. It was the first book by the eighteen-year-old writer, who used the sexually indecipherable pseudonym Marg. Yourcenar. Marguerite Yourcenar used to describe this prank with great pleasure. She enjoyed recalling it and intriguing interviewers with the bizarre anecdote. She even felt the need to retell it in her books. Before beginning "The First Evening," therefore, one should reread the lengthy description of the event in *Souvenirs pieux (Dear Departed)*.

"In 1927 or 1928, my father opened a drawer and pulled out a dozen manuscript pages, in that wider-than-longer format on which Proust wrote his drafts and which can no longer be found, I believe, in stationery stores today. It was the first chapter of a novel begun around 1904, which he had not continued. Other than translating a few poems, it was his only literary attempt.

"A worldly man, whom he called Georges de ———, probably in his thirties, was traveling to Switzerland with the young woman he had married that very morning in Versailles. During the writing, Michel had inadvertently changed their destination, making them spend the night in Cologne. The young woman was worried about being separated from her mother for the first time; the husband, who had only just, and with a sense of relief, broken with his mistress, thought of her now with sorrow and tenderness. Georges was touched by the naive innocence of his very young traveling companion: he thought how, in a moment, that very evening, he would cause her to lose this fragile quality and

would transform her into a woman like all others.
The somewhat strained politeness, the shy and
tender considerations of these two people newly
joined for life, who find themselves for the first time
alone with one another in a private compartment,
were well portrayed, as was the somewhat embar-
rassing choice of a room with only one bed in a Cologne hotel. Georges, leaving his wife to prepare
herself for the night, out of sheer boredom strikes up
a conversation with the waiter in the smoking room.
Half-an-hour later, avoiding the elevator for fear of
being subjected to the scrutinizing eye of the elevator boy, he climbs the stairs, enters the room, which
is bathed in the weak glow of the nightlamp, and,
taking his clothes off one by one, performs with a
mixture of impatience and disillusionment the motions he had so often made in the company of casual
women, and wishes for something else, not knowing
exactly what.

"I was charmed by the exact tone of this story
with no literary pretensions. In those days I was writing my first novel, *Alexis*. From time to time I'd
read a few pages to Michel: he was an excellent lis-
tener, capable of completely penetrating a character

so different from his own. I think it was my description of Alexis's wedding that made him recall his past efforts.

"A few magazines had already published, here and there, a story of mine, an essay or a poem. He suggested that I publish this story under my own name. This offer, extraordinary however one considers it, was typical of the sort of casual intimacy that existed between us. I refused, for the simple reason that I was not the author of those pages. He insisted:

"'You'll make them yours by fixing them up in whatever way you like. They need a title, and they have to be padded a little. I would rather enjoy it if they did appear after all these years, but at my age I'm not going to submit a manuscript to an editorial board.'

"The ploy tempted me. Just as Michel showed no surprise at seeing me write Alexis's confession, he didn't find it in the least incongruous to place under my pen the story of a wedding night set in 1900. In the eyes of this man who was always saying that nothing human should be alien to us, age and sex were but secondary contingencies in the field of literary creation. Problems that would later leave my critics perplexed were of no consequence to him."

In light of what Marguerite Yourcenar was to become, one can easily imagine the exultation with which this twenty-four-year-old woman must have followed the tracks of the man who had seemingly experienced everything, or almost everything, and who had married probably for reasons of social propriety, mingling an insatiable curiosity about women with infinite condescension, against a background of profound disinterest: "He felt no more desire for her than for any other woman." One can see, through the text rewritten by Marguerite Yourcenar, the deep joy she felt in recasting phrases that gave her the sense, even though she had not yet lived, of having lived life to the full. "Was she really simple-minded enough," the story says of the young bride, "to expect a secret revelation from life, when all life has to offer us is incessant nagging?" Marguerite Yourcenar was certainly not going to be satisfied with merely copying out her father's story. She left out the undressing (the clothes taken off "one by one") described in the original, less for reasons of prudery (which was not one of her traits) than to preserve a

silence, a sort of suspense—to leave the scene incon-
clusive. Nevertheless, she wasn't convinced of having bettered the text, and some fifty years later she
was severely critical of the work, recognizing its ba-
nalities and commonplaces.

"I don't know which of the two of us chose the title 'The First Evening' for that brief text, and I am
still not certain whether I like it or not. In any case,
it was I who pointed out to Michel that this first chapter of an unfinished novel, now transformed into a
short story, ended, so to speak, in mid-telling. We
looked for a concluding incident. One of us came up
with a telegram delivered by the hotel porter just as
Georges is about to walk upstairs—a telegram announcing the suicide of his uncertainly regretted mistress. The incident didn't seem unlikely: I didn't
realize that it transformed these pages, whose great-
est merit lay in their vagueness, into something
banal. This time we set the wedding night in Montreux, where we happened to be during the rewrit-
ing. My 'padding' consisted in making Georges into
an intellectual always ready to plunge into a deep
meditation on whatever subject came his way; something which, contrary to what I thought, did nothing

to improve the text. Recast along these lines, the story was sent off to a magazine, which rejected it after the usual delay, and then to another, which accepted it for publication, but by then my father was already dead. The little text appeared a year later and received a modest literary award, which would have amused Michel and also have pleased him."

The story was in fact awarded second prize, worth two thousand francs, from the subscribers to the *Revue de France.* As usual, the account Marguerite Yourcenar gives of it in *Dear Departed* is somewhat inaccurate. The remarkable detail invented by father and daughter in order to provide an ending for the story—the telegram announcing the mistress's suicide—is given to Georges not at the foot of the stairs but in his room, which allows the moment of going to bed to be postponed and the end of the story to be reached without the scene's taking place. If the text is appealing to a present-day reader curious about Yourcenar's personality, it didn't lack biographical interest for Yourcenar herself. In *Dear Departed*, she asks what traces of real life Michel de Crayencour might have left in the text he believed to be the bare bones of a novel.

"I've sometimes wondered what elements of real life might be found in that 'First Evening.' It appears that Monsieur de C. had made use of the true novelist's privilege of inventing, relying only occasionally on his own experience. Of Michel's two wives, neither the first, Berthe, full of self-determination and daring, nor Fernande, more complex and, in any case, an orphan, in the least resembled the young bride so attached to her mother. The second honeymoon, the only one that might concern us here, was far from bringing together for the first time, in the buffeted intimacy of a private compartment, two people who hardly knew one another, and it is doubtful whether Michel, in order to marry Fernande, abandoned an official mistress: on the contrary, it seems that the solitude of a winter spent in Lille persuaded him to attempt this new adventure. The private confession can be found, rather, in the tender and easy sensuality of the story's tone, in that vague notion that this is what life is about, and that perhaps life might be better in some other way. *Mutatis mutandi*, we might imagine Monsieur de C. in some Grand Hotel on the Italian or French Riviera, still not too busy in early November, spending a long

half-hour in the smoking room or on the rather
damp terrace overlooking the sea, where, with spend-
thrift concern, the staff have lighted only a few of
the large white porcelain globes that in those days
used to adorn the terraces of the best establishments.
Like his character, he would have preferred the
stairs to the elevator. Setting foot on the brass-
framed red carpet that leads to what the Italians call
the 'noble floor,' he climbs the stairs neither too
quickly nor too slowly, asking himself how it will all
end."

In all of Yourcenar's comments on the four-
handed composition of "The First Evening," we can
perceive a desire to remain vague, to preserve a delightful uncertainty about "who did what." We don't
know who came up with the title, who suggested the
ending. And yet she strongly asserts her personal
"contribution," that of turning Georges into an intellectual, bringing him closer to her father's own character (even if this "did not improve him"), as if she
wished to transform the story into a posthumous au-
tobiographical fragment. So she raises the question
of a biographical source regarding the text Monsieur
de Crayencourt had submitted to her. Even if she

doesn't say so, we can imagine what it was that at-
tracted her most to her father's words and to the
possibility of making them hers. In the exercise in lu-
cidity set out for her by an older man she found
something that was to remain a constant concern to
the end of her life: the banishment of sentimentality,
bathos, moralizing, and a preference for being read
as a cynic rather than being accused of inanity. Also,
"The First Evening" allowed Marguerite Yourcenar
to place herself at a certain distance from the general-
ity of women: "So many women think of nothing."
Or, at least, from the stereotype of women, like the
timid young bride, shy, credulous, in a word, rather
dumb, the girl "destined to become banal when
she became a woman." Like an echo, the reader can
hear the "Not a chance!" of a woman who rejects
convention. She will not be "robbed of her grace,
deformed, shriveled down to all the pettiness of conjugal life." She will never share the immense credulity of women, in matters either of sex or of sickness
and maternity. "Would she have a child? Of course
she'd have a child. He tried to imagine her pregnant.
So he'd give her a child she'd delight in, even if it
made her ugly and sick." As she reads these lines—

and agrees with them, since she publishes them under her own name—Marguerite Yourcenar sets out
to prove that one can be a woman *otherwise*. She'll
succeed.

"An Evil Spell" lacks the delightful ambiguities
of "The First Evening." Marguerite Yourcenar herself, in the chronology established for the first volume of her works in Gallimard's deluxe series of
classics, "Bibliothèque de la Pléiade," places the writing of this story—"a realistic evocation of Italian
customs"—in 1927, even though it first appeared six
years later. The farther back we place it among her
juvenilia, the more excusable does its conventional
character appear. It has been written about frequently by certain specialists, and linked to the subject of "Yourcenar's Mediterranean." It is true that
the characters are Italian and that this tale of freeing
someone from a spell is obviously Mediterranean.
But is that enough? Other specialists, those who
deal with Yourcenar and her use of history, stress its
allusions to fascism—and to the communists who
are persecuted and forced to escape from Italy. They
also stress, pertinently but perhaps a little too exces-
sively, "her historical technique," which supposedly

underpins the text. Perhaps the specialists have paid too much attention to this slight narrative exercise.

And yet, rereading it in the context of this volume allows us to see it in a new light. The ceremony used to counteract the spell cast on Amanda, who suffers from tuberculosis as a result of the sorcery, is performed in the midst of a group of credulous women by a "disenchanter," Cattaneo d'Aigues. As expected, one of the women, Algenare, is shown to be guilty through her own agitation and denial; she's the one responsible for casting spells. But how did she manage it? Cattaneo wants to know. Piercing the heart of a bull? Burying a lemon under the threshold? "No," says Algenare, "I wished it . . . just wished it . . ." "Ah, then you're very powerful." Of course: the woman who succeeds in stepping out of the women's circle (and for whom Yourcenar, not without humor, expresses her admiration) can only be a witch. As in the story's final words, "the stars drew for her, in large trembling strokes, the giant letters of the witches' alphabet."

These rediscovered texts, assembled almost by chance so as to rescue them from being scattered and to place them before a wider public than that of

researchers and specialists, ultimately form a youth-
ful triptych on the subject of credulity. Since her ado-
lescence, Marguerite Yourcenar had been striving to
avoid that weakness—a weakness distorted in the
discourse of men, who are so often credulous themselves, into a charming trait of the female character.

Useful as documents (literary in the case of "A
Blue Tale," foreshadowing a whole aspect of Yourcenar's work, sketching out a style; biographical in
the case of "The First Evening," where we can continue to reflect on the father's fundamental ploy, in
which not everything becomes clear; historical in
the case of "An Evil Spell"), they demonstrate Yourcenar's taste—and talent—for the short form. Com-
menting on *Oriental Tales*, Matthieu Galey described
it as "a separate construction in Marguerite Yourcenar's oeuvre, as precious as a chapel in a vast palace." These words also describe most of Yourcenar's
other short pieces, even those that are unpolished—
and that she herself judged harshly—or conventional, such as "An Evil Spell." Indeed, both the fail-
ings and the promising aspects are revealing. These
"little texts," which are both sketches and works of
full range, now fulfill a double function in Yource-

nar's oeuvre. A restrospective reading will reveal traces of a continuity, since the author expresses here a radical break from her "pre-writing age." Through these texts—of which "The First Evening" is emblematic—runs the path of no return from filial and human sentiment to a sensibility that links Yourcenar to a lineage both creative and cultural.

JOSYANE SAVIGNEAU

A
BLUE
TALE

THE MERCHANTS from Europe were sitting on the deck, facing the blue sea, in the indigo shade of the sails heavily patched with gray. The sun constantly changed position among the riggings, and the rolling of the ship made it bounce like a ball through a net with too loose a mesh. The ship kept turning to avoid the reef, and the watchful pilot stroked his blue chin.

The merchants disembarked at sunset onto a dock paved with white marble. Bluish veins ran across the surface of the great stone slabs, which had formerly served as paneling for the temples. The shadows the merchants cast behind them on the road as they walked toward dusk were larger, slimmer, and not as dark as in the midday sun, tinged with a very pale blue that evoked the rings beneath the eyelids of a sick woman. Blue inscriptions quivered on the white domes of the mosques like tattoos on the delicate breast of a girl, and from time to time a turquoise, pulled down by its own weight, fell with a dull sound onto a carpet of a faded, downy blue.

No sooner had the moon risen than it began to roam the cone-shaped tombs of the graveyard like a ghoul. The sky was blue as a mermaid's scaly tail, and to the Greek merchant the bare mountains circling the horizon bore a faint resemblance to the blue, shorn haunches of the centaurs.

All the stars concentrated their light into the women's palace. The merchants entered the courtyard to shield themselves from the sea wind, but the frightened women refused to allow them inside, and in vain they skinned their fingers beating the steel gates, which gleamed like the blade of a sword. The cold was so bitter that the Dutch merchant lost all five toes on his left foot, and two of the Italian merchant's fingers on his right hand were bitten off by a tortoise that he had mistaken, in the dark, for a plain, uncut lapis lazuli. At last a tall black man came out of the palace in tears, and told them that every night the ladies-in-waiting rejected his love because his skin was not quite dark enough. The Greek merchant won his goodwill with the gift of a talisman fashioned out of dried blood and graveyard earth, and the Nubian led them into a large room the color of ultramarine, warning the women not to speak too loudly for fear of waking the camels in their stables and disturbing the snakes that suck the moonlight milk.

The merchants opened their trunks under the curious gaze of the servant girls, in the midst of blue-scented vapors, but none of the ladies-in-waiting answered their questions, and the princesses did not accept their gifts. In a hall of golden panels a Chinese woman dressed in orange called them impostors because the rings they offered her became invisible as soon as they touched her yellow skin. They failed to notice a woman dressed in black sitting at the end of the corridor, and when they inadvertently trod on a fold of her dress, she cursed them in the Tartar tongue in the name of the blue sky, in the Turkish tongue in the name of the sun, and in the tongue of the desert in the name of the sands. In a room hung with cobwebs they drew no answer from a woman dressed in gray who was constantly feeling herself to ascertain her own existence; in a ruby-colored room they fled from a woman dressed in red who was losing all her blood from a deep wound in her breast but who seemed not to notice because her dress showed not the slightest stain.

Finally they sought refuge in the kitchens and argued among themselves about the best way to reach the cave of sapphires. They were incessantly interrupted by the water carriers, and a mangy dog came and licked the blue stumps of the Italian merchant's fingers. Eventually they saw a young slave woman emerge from the cellar stairs, carrying chunks of ice heaped in a bowl of cloudy glass. Without looking, she put down the bowl on a column of air, thus freeing her hands to raise them in salutation to her forehead, tattooed with the star of the magi. Her blue-black hair fell from her temples to her shoulders; her clear eyes gazed at the world through two tears, and her mouth was nothing but a bluish bruise. Her dress, of lavender cloth faded from too many washings, was badly torn at the knees because she was in the habit of endlessly kneeling in prayer.

Since she was a deafmute, it mattered little that she didn't understand their language. She nodded solemnly when they pointed first at the color of her eyes and then at her footsteps in the dust of the passageway. The Greek merchant offered her his talismans: she refused them like a woman who has everything, but with the smile of a woman in despair; the Dutch merchant handed her a pouchful of jewels, but she curtseyed, spreading her ragged dress with both hands, and they could not tell whether she thought herself too poor or too rich for such splendors.

She raised the latch of a door with a blade of grass, and they found themselves inside a round courtyard like the bottom of a pail, full to the brim with the cold morning light. With her little finger the young woman opened a second door, which led out into the open, and in single file they made their way toward the interior of the island along a path edged by rows of aloe bushes. The merchants' shadows clung to their heels, small and black as vipers. Only the young woman had no shadow, which made them wonder whether she was a ghost.

The blue hills in the distance turned black, brown, and gray as they drew near; but the merchant from the Touraine did not lose heart and sang songs from his homeland to keep his spirits up. The Castilian merchant was stung twice by a scorpion; his legs swelled up as far as his knees and turned the color of ripe eggplant, but he felt no pain and walked with an even surer and more solemn tread than the others, as if supported by two thick pillars of blue basalt. The Irish merchant wept because pale drops of blood clung like pearls to the young woman's heels as she walked barefoot over shards of china and broken glass.

They had to crawl on their knees into the cave, which opened to the world through a narrow mouth with cracked lips. But its deep throat was unexpectedly spacious, and once their eyes had befriended the darkness, they discovered everywhere fragments of sky between the fissures of the rocks. A pristine lake occupied the center of the underground chamber. When the Italian merchant threw in a chip to measure its depth, no sound was heard; instead, bubbles formed on the surface as if a mermaid, suddenly awoken, had breathed out all the air from her blue lungs. The Greek merchant dipped thirsty hands into the water, which colored them up to the wrists like the boiling liquid in a dyer's vat, but he failed to catch the sapphires floating like schools of nautilus on these waters denser than the ocean. Then the young woman undid her long tresses and dipped her hair into the water, catching the sapphires as if in the silky mesh of a dark net. First she called to the Dutch merchant, who stuffed them in his leggings, and then to the merchant from the Touraine, who stashed them away in his hat. The Greek merchant filled a goatskin that he always carried over his shoulder, and the Castilian merchant, his hands damp with sweat, ripped off his leather gloves and from now on wore them hanging from his neck like severed hands. When it was the Irish merchant's turn, the lake bore no more sapphires, and the young woman took the glass pendant from her neck, commanding him through signs to place it on his heart.

They crawled out of the cave, and the young woman asked the Irish merchant to help her roll a large stone across the opening. Then she made a seal out of clay and a strand of her hair. The road seemed to them longer than it had that morning, and the Castilian merchant, whose poisoned legs had begun to cause him pain, staggered along blaspheming the name of the Mother of God. The Dutch merchant, hungry, tried to break off the blue gourds of ripe figs, but hundreds of bees buried in the succulent flesh stung him deeply on his hands and neck.

When they reached the foot of the walls, they made a detour to avoid the guards. Without a sound, they headed toward the port of the mermaid hunters, which was always deserted, for it had been many years since mermaids were hunted in that country. Their ship was floating idly on the waters, tied to a bronze toe, which was all that was left of a colossal statue erected to honor a god whose name no one remembered. On the dock, the young woman tried to say farewell to the merchants by placing her hands on

her heart, but the Greek merchant grabbed her by the
wrists and dragged her on board the ship because he
planned to sell her to the Venetian prince of Negro-
ponte, who loved only women who were crippled or
wounded. The deafmute allowed herself to be taken
away without resistance, and her tears, falling on the
planks of the dock, turned into aquamarines, so that
from then onward her kidnappers contrived to make
her weep.

They stripped her and lashed her to the tallest
mast. So white was her body that on that clear island
night it became the ship's beacon. When they had
finished their game of spillikins, the merchants went
down into the cabin to sleep. At dawn, the Dutch
merchant, tormented by desire, climbed up to the
bridge and approached the prisoner with the intention
of violating her. But she had disappeared; the empty
cords hung from the black trunk of the mast like a
belt that was too long, and in the spot where her thin
soft feet had stood, nothing remained but a handful of
aromatic herbs from which rose a trail of blue smoke.

On the following days the sea was calm, and the sun's rays falling on that seaweed-colored expanse sizzled like white-hot iron suddenly plunged into cold water. The gangrenous legs of the Castilian merchant were blue as the mountains glimpsed on the horizon, and rivulets of white-streaked blood ran along the planks of the bridge into the sea. When his suffering became intolerable, he drew a large triangular dagger from his belt and cut off his two poisoned legs at the thighs. Exhausted, he died at dawn, having left his sapphires to the merchant from Bâle because he was his mortal enemy.

After a week had gone by, they stopped at Smyrna, and the merchant from the Touraine, fearful of the sea, had himself set ashore with the intention of continuing his journey on the back of a strong mule. An Armenian banker exchanged his sapphires for ten thousand gold pieces stamped with the profile of Prester John; they were perfectly round, and the merchant from the Touraine joyfully loaded them on thirteen mules. But when he returned to Angers after seven years' travel, he learned that Prester John's coins had no currency in his homeland.

In Ragusa, the Dutch merchant bartered his sapphires for a pitcher of beer sold on the quay, but soon afterward he spat out the bland, flat liquid, which lacked the taste he remembered from the taverns of Amsterdam. In Venice, the Italian merchant disembarked and had himself made Doge, but died, murdered the day after his betrothal to the Sea. As for the Greek merchant, he tied his sapphires to a long thread and hung them over the side of the ship so that the waves might enhance the fine blue of the stones. The humid gems turned to liquid and added nothing to the booty of the sea but a few drops of transparent water, and the Greek merchant consoled himself by catching fish, which he cooked in hot ashes.

On the evening of the twenty-seventh day they were attacked by a pirate ship. The merchant from Bâle swallowed his sapphires to save them from the pirates' greed, and died torn by pains in his entrails. The Greek merchant threw himself into the sea and was rescued by a dolphin, which led him to Tinos. The Irish merchant, felled by blows, was left for dead on the ship among the corpses and the empty sacks, and no one bothered to divest him of the blue glass pendant. After thirty days, the drifting ship entered on its own accord the port of Dublin, and the Irishman disembarked to beg a piece of bread.

It was raining. The sloping roofs of the houses seemed like great mirrors for holding captive the ghosts of the dead light. The uneven road was scattered with puddles; the sky, a dirty brown, was so murky that the Angels themselves would not have ventured out of the House of God. The streets were completely deserted; a traveling haberdasher stall, wreathed with shoelaces and beige stockings, stood abandoned at the side of the road, under an open umbrella. The kings and bishops sculpted on the cathedral's portal did nothing to prevent the rain from falling on their crowns or tiaras, and Saint Mary Magdalene bore the rain on her naked breasts.

The disheartened merchant sat down under the

portal beside a young beggar-maid. She was so poor that her body, blue with cold, could be glimpsed through her ragged gray dress; her knees knocked faintly against each other. In her chilblained fingers she was holding a crust of bread, which the merchant begged her to give him for the love of God. She gave it to him at once.

The merchant wanted to offer her the blue glass pendant, the only thing he had to give in exchange for the bread. But he searched in vain in his pockets, around his neck, and among the beads of his rosary. And he burst into tears, for he had nothing left to remind him of the color of the sky and the changing tints of the sea in which he had almost perished.

He sighed a deep sigh, and as the twilight and the cold fog had begun to thicken around them, she drew close to him to lend him warmth. He asked her for news of the country, and she replied in the dialect of the village he had left as a child. So he parted the disheveled hair that covered her face, but the beggar-maid's skin was so grimy that the rain traced white

furrows on it, and the merchant realized with horror
that she was blind, and that her left eye was already
half-hidden behind a sinister white film. Yet he rested
his head on her ragged knees and fell asleep feeling
comforted, for her right eye, though sightless, appeared somehow to be of a miraculous blue.

THE
FIRST
EVENING

I

THEY WERE on their honeymoon. The train sped toward the banality of Switzerland; sitting in the reserved compartment, they held hands. Silence weighed heavily upon them. They loved one another, or at least they thought they did, but their loves, so different from one another, only helped them understand how little they had in common. She was confident, almost happy, yet scared of the new life that was about to begin, which would turn her into a different woman, a woman she was surprised not to know and was attempting to imagine, like a stranger to whom she must henceforth become accustomed. He, more experienced, was all too conscious of the fragility of the emotion that had driven him toward this girl, destined to become banal when she became a woman. What he had liked in her was precisely what was bound to disappear: her candor, her astonishments, the atmosphere of pristine youth in which he had met her. He imagined her robbed of her grace, deformed, shriveled down to all the pettiness of conjugal life which would transform her into a woman like all others. A moment ago he had been on the point of taking her into his arms and destroying her. An instant would have been enough: relaxing his embrace, he would have felt in his heart that he had committed murder, and passion would not have granted him extenuating circumstances since, after all, he felt no desire for her. Or, at least, he felt no more desire for her than for any other woman.

He wondered what she was thinking. Was she having similar thoughts? Or, rather, was she thinking at all? So many women think of nothing. Was she really simple-minded enough to expect a secret revelation from life, when all life has to offer us is incessant nagging? Would she end up by begging from a lover the happiness he would not have given her, that no one else would give her either, because it wouldn't be his to give? Did she imagine one carried happiness in one's wallet, like a check that needs only to be endorsed? Checks can be issued without funds. He almost laughed at the thought that in the future she might accuse him of fraud.

He raised his head and looked at himself in the mirror. The clothes he was wearing, which seemed too contrived for traveling, made him uncomfortable with himself. No doubt she thought him handsome. This lack of taste annoyed him. He saw, as if the train were crossing the landscape of his future, the long series of monotonous days during which the arrival of a friend would be her only distraction, the evenings in which he would gladly join the circle of the men talking about other women with a coarseness he'd relish, the same coarseness, no doubt, with which they would speak about his wife when he wasn't present. Would she have a child? Of course she'd have a child. He tried to imagine her pregnant. So he'd give her a child she'd delight in, even if it made her ugly and sick; a child for whom he'd feel an indulgent, amused affection as long as the child remained a child, for later he would cause them innumerable worries. They would worry about his health, be nervous during his exams, plot ways to help his career or find him a wife. They would probably disagree on how to bring him up. They would quarrel, like everyone else.

Or would he allow himself to be gently possessed by that conjugal, paternal blindness he had so often mocked in others, overcome (one is always overcome) by life, which tends to pour all beings into identical molds?

Yet none of this might happen.

There are other possibilities, moments of happiness or of sadness that one has neglected to invite, and that seek revenge by arriving all of a sudden, unannounced.

She might die. He imagined her dead, lying in her coffin under a veil of white gauze; he saw himself, dressed in black, possessing, in the eyes of the fifty-year-old women, the prestige of suffering a misfortune. And black suited him. His own insensibility annoyed him, as if he were already tired of mourning her. And he might be the one who died. He would die of typhoid fever during a trip to Algeria or Spain, and she would have nursed him with the kind of tireless devotion that later makes a good impression on men who might consider marrying a widow. But she would not remarry. She loved him. Rather, not having loved anyone before, she imagined she loved him. For her, loving him was almost a necessity, since she had married him. There was no other way out. If he died in Algeria, she would go back alone, to her mother. She had never traveled by herself. He reproached himself for leaving her on her own, as if he were certain that all this would happen, and as if he were truly responsible. Was it not enough for him to look after himself, without taking on this unknown girl as well? It would have been better for her to marry someone else. He should have made it clear to her. He felt a growing tenderness. He came to his senses. He watched her with gentle emotion, and a great despondency overcame him.

II

They were pulling into Chambéry. Having nothing to say, she hunted for something to ask, like an object that isn't important in itself but becomes important through our obstinate pursuit of it. She opened her handbag. In it were a Saint Christopher medal and a Sacred Heart medal. She thought of showing them to him, then imagined he would find them ridiculous and, not to let him think she had acted without a purpose, merely pulled out her handkerchief. She peered at the landscape: it was not as beautiful as she had pictured it, but she kept embellishing it by an unconscious effort of the imagination, for she didn't want this day, even in its slightest details, to be inferior to the one she had promised herself. That was why, a little earlier, she claimed to have enjoyed the mediocre meal in the restaurant car, and expressed admiration for the delicate pink of the silk lampshades.

Night was falling; only the tiny cabins of the signalmen could still be seen clearly along the tracks. For every house she saw, she told herself that he and she could live happily there, and this thought led her on to the furnishings and draperies that had been the cause of their first quarrels, at a time when they were merely engaged.

He, seeing the small windows lit in the gray-
ness of the twilight, asked himself, on the contrary,
whether the people living in those houses so impru-
dently built next to the tracks didn't envy the passen-
gers on the express train, and if they wouldn't finally
yield, some evening, to the temptation of climbing
aboard. Carried away, as if by the speeding train, toward a future of sensations foretold, he tried to draw
out the voluptuous sap of the present moment, to enjoy those moments that would never come back, fully
conscious of that which rendered them fragile. He
told himself, as he had frequently done before, and
often when in the company of other women, that
most of the moments that make up our life would be
delightful if they were not shadowed by the future or
the past, and that usually we are miserable only by
virtue of what we remember or what we expect. And
realizing once again that this girl had what people call
charm, that she probably loved him, that she was neither less intelligent nor less rich than is ordinarily de-
sirable, and that the weather had the good grace to be
fine, he decided to forge himself a state of happiness

out of all those diverse elements which would normally have satisfied most other men.

Their sudden entry into a tunnel forced them to speak, removing from their silence the pretext of the landscape.

"What are you thinking about, Georges?" she said.

He pulled himself together and answered with a sweetness that he himself found satisfying:

"About you of course, my dear."

And, while uttering this banal endearment, he realized that he was convincing himself of his love in the process of expressing it. He kissed her on the forehead, chastely. And so, too intimidated to find the courage to remain silent, she haphazardly inquired about the hotel where they'd be staying, the luggage, the time of arrival.

"And now we're so far from Grenoble," she said. "Poor Mother! I hope she's feeling a little more reassured. Did you notice, Georges, how sad she was when we left and how she held back her tears?"

This backward glance conjured up in him the image of another woman, his mistress, with whom he had broken up, and whom he was surprised still to remember. Had she wept? Had she held back her tears? Tired of that woman, as one can only be tired of that which one has loved too much, he had found it easy to leave her; breaking up with her, he had thought he could suppress the bitterness one feels at discovering, one evening, that one has aged enough to have a past. Where was she today? Now he recalled, with a certain tenderness, the experienced body of a mature woman and the calm eyes no longer startled by anything. He forgot the irritation he had felt at her faulty locutions, which pride prevented her from correcting so that they would not be thought involuntary, and which she had picked up in the days when she was the favorite of the district police. And how he had loathed her habit of humming popular songs when they were at the table! They had lived together for several years: he looked back at the time of their love with an indulgence born of incomplete memory,

and the certainty that those days would never return
made him less critical of the quality of happiness they
had given him. He had been to Italy and Provence
with her; certain episodes of that journey, which had
annoyed him, now moved him to tears, and the re-
membrance of those dazzling landscapes made him
detest, for a moment, the one that now lay before his
eyes. Then habit had settled in, and finally weariness.
The pleasure of breaking up was the only one she had
still been able to afford him; he had seen her cry on
the day he announced he was getting married, and he
had felt a certain vanity at still being loved enough to
make her suffer. He remembered, angrily, that wom-
en's tears tend to dry more quickly than their makeup;
she had been seen at an all-night restaurant with another man. He didn't hold it against her. They had
done well, both of them, to find a new beginning for
their lives. Whom had she chosen? No doubt someone she had laid eyes on much earlier, maybe even
during the time she had been his. He was enraged at
the thought that her tears might have been false; that

perhaps she had wanted him to break with her, had been lying in wait for weeks, hoping for an opportunity to leave him. He realized that he had to forget her by every possible means for a few hours, and with a violent effort he cast her away. He answered:

"Don't worry. Tomorrow you'll certainly find a letter from your mother waiting for you at the Grand Hotel. She was sad to see you leave, but in a month's time we'll be back and we'll be living very close to her."

And he exaggerated the affection he felt for his mother-in-law. He realized, however, that he hardly knew the lady. Then he thought, quite sensibly, that this isn't always a reason not to love someone.

She said to him:

"You're so kind!"

She took his hand. He felt flattered that she saw in him precisely the quality he lacked and was sorry he lacked. She leaned against his shoulder, wearied by a day that could not be added to the count of ordinary days, and that she would identify in her

memory with her wedding dress, as something va-
porous and formal, something planned far in ad-
vance and not looked at twice. He put his arm
around her shoulders and kissed her on the neck.
Her hair was blond; so was the hair of the other
woman, but since she colored it with henna, it was
of a different shade. He remembered telling her that
he'd never be able to love a dark-haired woman,
and this faithfulness in the midst of his inconstancy
seemed to him strangely sad.

They spoke of trivial things, about her parents,
about things that took on a hidden, almost symbolic
meaning for him. He realized that from now on he
would have to interest himself in this family which
wasn't his own—he who for so long had boasted of
not having one. He realized that he'd be moved by
their bereavements, happy at their promotions and
births; that each of these unforeseeable events would
touch him and change him, however slightly, and
that, just as very old couples grow to resemble one
another like sister and brother, he would assume these

people's mannerisms, their tastes in cooking, perhaps even their political opinions. He accepted this. He was thirty-five years old. What had he done until then? He had painted a few canvases, which had not turned out as well as he might have wished, and had had some financial success, which he had not enjoyed as much as he thought he would. Like a swimmer who decides to sink to the bottom and so abandons himself with a certain gentleness to the water's suction, he felt as though he were falling without resistance into that easy, ordinary life that others thought adequate. He would continue to paint, to amuse himself; he would busy himself with the administration of his funds; they would entertain. He imagined a commonplace happiness, proper, suited to all those family traditions he believed were his from birth, legitimate yet sensuous. He pictured vacations by the sea, summer in the country, children on a lawn, his wife's open housecoat as she sat on the balcony pouring out the morning tea, and the richer, fuller, more satisfied beauty she would then possess. Because the motion of the train had given her a headache, she had taken off her hat; he thought her hair was badly done and that it would have to be changed. Laure's hairdresser had better taste. He'd take her to him.

He felt cold. He stood up to close the window, but realizing that he had to look after her at all costs, he sat down again and asked her whether the draft didn't bother her. Then he occupied himself with her vanity case and even tried to open one of the little bottles, which had been too tightly fastened. The evening spread slowly, langorously, opening up wide like a woman's fan: the vapidity of the moment made him think back to the early days of their courtship. All of a sudden she seemed to him infinitely rich and precious, full of all future possibilities that depended solely on her, as if she carried within her, like a child only she could bring forth, their life to come. Their conversation, which had reassured him because it had entertained him, became intermittent, riddled with silences: he was afraid that this brittle barrier of words set up between him and his thoughts would suddenly

give way, leaving him alone with himself—in other
words, with the other.

III

The train stopped for customs; they were relieved by
the break in their transient immobility. The doors
opened: he stepped down first, held his hands out to
her. She jumped onto the platform with a light tread
that reminded him of the Andromeda on a bas-relief
in Rome. The comparison flattered him: she was already one of his possessions. The formalities were
short; the officials were discreetly considerate with
the young woman; his male vanity was pleased and
he felt less sad.

A few hours later, they arrived in Montreux. The
bus drove them to the hotel. Under the awning, bellboys picked up their luggage; one of the managers
showed them several rooms and asked if they wished
to have a double or two singles. As they took their
time to answer, he discreetly walked away. Georges
looked at his wife; their eyes met.

"Shall we take this one?" he asked.

"Yes, of course, if you wish," she answered.

It was a large room with a double bed, so white it seemed almost indecent. The manager returned.

"This one will suit us," Georges told him.

He thought he noticed a hint of mockery in the man's obsequiousness.

The luggage was brought up. She was standing in front of the mirror, slowly taking off her gloves, her hat, her coat; and one could sense that these motions, which she must have performed so often in her own former bedroom, gave her the reassuring feeling of continuing her everyday habits. Georges oversaw the placing of the trunks, the lifting of the straps. Then the bellboys left; they were alone. He looked at her: she was tall and thin, like a girl who had grown too fast. The mirror that transformed her into two identical women stripped her of the privilege of being unique. She was combing her hair, and her upraised arms made her young breasts stand out. He took hold of her without saying a word, pulled her head backward, and kissed her hard on the lips. She accepted his kiss without returning it. All she said was:

"Please . . ."

And he didn't know whether she was speaking out of a sense of propriety or shyness. He drew away. After a moment, he asked:

"You're not cross with me?"

She answered no, with a gesture. He would almost have wished that she didn't love him, so that he might experience the pleasure of winning her or conquering her. She had started to unfold her clothes, which made him think of her body. Having nothing to do, he felt more uncomfortable than she did. He said he was going down to the lobby to look at the evening papers; with a timidity that made him irritated with himself, he added that he'd be back in an hour. She nodded in acquiescence, which he interpreted as a caress. He approached her, kissed her less warmly, and left.

In the lobby, he took out a cigar, lit it, and sat down. His mind felt heavy, yet seemed empty; he

tried to remember if their room was on the fourth or
the fifth floor; he thought, with distaste, of one of his
unfinished canvases; he discovered he had forgotten
the name of a certain character in Balzac; he tried
to recall it by running through the letters of the alphabet; finally he concluded that it was of no importance. Then he remembered: Laure had just been con-
tracted by a film company to play Madame de Sérizy.
Who was Madame de Sérizy in Balzac's novels? He
changed seats, sat down at a table to look at the papers, and read the leader in the *Journal de Genève* and
reread it, concentrating, trying to understand. The
latest news informed him that a pilot had been given
an enthusiastic welcome after crossing the Atlantic:
he would not have wanted to be in the pilot's place;
that a smallpox epidemic had broken out in Germany:
he had been vaccinated; that the De Beers stock had
dropped a thousand francs: he had a few shares. He
put the paper aside. He resisted the temptation to go
upstairs immediately so as to catch her in the midst of
her preparations for the night, and he promised him-

self he wouldn't leave until he had finished his cigar. He walked up and down the lobby, tried to show some interest in the posters on the walls; to have something to do he ordered a cup of tea, and snapped at the waiter who took his time to serve him. The clock showed eleven. Standing at the entrance to the lobby, he watched the women cut out in black through the transparency of their gowns. Laure's gowns were expensive; he congratulated himself on having broken up with her, recalling the last bills he had paid. He saw, once again, her naked foot on the edge of a bed, like an *Empire* wall lamp cut in marble instead of gilded bronze. Overcome by the image, he tried to force the emotions still roused by his memory, attempting to attain in the new woman's presence that degree of passion which he despaired of achieving. A physical weakness took hold of him, then left him. The clock showed a quarter past. He glanced at the mirror and found himself absurdly pale. Forgoing the elevator so as not to be subjected to a conversation with the elevator boy, he climbed the stairs slowly, almost with effort. The exertion of walking up four flights lent a pretext to the beating of his heart. At the door of their room he stopped, wondering whether to knock. He knocked gently, then louder; no answer came. After a moment he turned the handle and slowly opened the door, which was not locked. The room was in half-darkness, the lights were out; only an open window, at the far end, linked the room to the world and the night. He went in and saw her lying down, pressed against the wall, lost in a bed that seemed empty to him, so thin had she made herself in order to take up as little space as possible.

"It's me," he said.

Without a sound, he came up to her, bent over the bed, whispered:

"Will you make a little room for me, Jeanne?"

She drew her hand out from under the covers and gave it to him. He walked away and started to undress.

The action seemed to him desperately banal. How many times had he performed the same gesture in casual encounters, encounters without a future, without a past. It was always the same scene, the same setting: a hotel room in which he undressed while a woman waited for him in bed. It pained him to see that the circumstances were so sadly similar; it surprised him that he should have expected anything else. He smiled to think that one becomes accustomed to everything, even to living, and that in ten years' time he would be suffering the misfortune of being happy. The lake, with its illuminated ships and its mountains dotted with houses in which the lights were still burning, stood out in the night like an immense postcard with artistic pretensions. He went onto the balcony and looked out at it all.

He realized that it was only a small corner of the world. Behind those mountains were other plains, other countries, other rooms, other men hesitating by the edge of a bed in which a woman would give herself for the very first time; others leaning on the windowsill, having at last decided to tear themselves away from the flesh, having suddenly understood that happiness doesn't lie in the depths of a body. He felt a strange kinship with those men, at this very moment leaning out of a window open onto the night, as if on the edge of a cliff from which they cannot leap. Because one doesn't plunge into the night. Men and women come and go, within a space they themselves have created, a place whose limits are determined by their houses and their furniture and which has no longer anything in common with what the universe used to be. They carry their space with them wherever they go, and since that evening they had chosen to sail in brightly lit ships, the Lake of Geneva seemed nothing more than a boardwalk, or a lovers' lane. Yet there it was. It existed by itself, indifferent to all the links between it and man, and Georges understood, with an emotion that brought him close to tears, that the beauty of this hackneyed landscape consisted precisely in resisting all the interpretations of a passerby, content with just being, and, however hard one might try to to reach it, remaining elsewhere.

Was it possible that man, having thought about it for so long, had not yet understood that beauty is ineffable and that neither beings nor things can be fathomed? People sailed away, on that lake kind enough to be calm, in those bright ships that spoiled the night, and they boasted of being happy. They weren't disturbed by the thought that this lake, closed in on all sides, offered no exit; they would be satisfied to sail back and forth forever at the foot of those mountains, which concealed something from them. These people knew that rivers, like roads, lead only to foreseeable places picked out on maps, and that each river is but the continuation of another. They felt neither fear nor desire to be elsewhere; perhaps there was no elsewhere, just as there was no exit. There were just men and women sailing round and round in a circle they couldn't break out of, on a lake whose surface they barely grazed, beneath a sky that was closed to them.

Georges remembered having read in a geology textbook (the name of which he tried for a painful moment to recall) that this mountain gorge, into which rivers and mountain streams had accumulated their deposits for thousands of years, would one day be filled and turn into a plain, and the idea that this beauty would one day perish consoled him for being a mere mortal. He wondered, laughing silently, if many men had thoughts like these on their wedding night, and at the same time he was disgusted at priding himself on his airs of intelligence. The gaudy ships, continuing their rounds in the night, which they were steadily repelling, reminded him of a pair of lovers, glimpsed in Venice, in the intimacy of a gondola, whose vulgar exhibition of happiness had seemed to him a public affront to propriety. This repugnant memory steered him back to thoughts of pleasure, as if there had been a secret complicity between him and those unknown lovers. Lucid enough to witness within himself the growth of passion—which he had, until then, feared absent—he took it upon himself to have his expectation increase deliciously, enjoying in anticipation that sensation which would, for a few seconds, erase all thought, even if in the end it would bring on new complications. He asked himself if Jeanne, still awake, was also waiting, and what fear or what love was mingled with her expectation.

IV

Someone knocked discreetly. He opened the door: the impersonal, mechanical voice of a bellboy announced:

"A telegram for you, sir."

Rather than switch on the lamp, he held the piece of blue paper out and read it by the light in the corridor. He heard Jeanne, from the other side of the room, ask what the matter was; he heard himself answer that he had just received a message from his broker. Assuring her that it was of no importance, he locked the door, crossed the room in order to close the windows, and after a moment's hesitation leaned out again over the balustrade, which was now damp from the night air.

In his pajama pocket he could feel the bulge of

the crumpled paper. He analyzed himself sternly, trying to discern what emotion had swept over him; the increasingly clear realization that his feeling was one of relief, and that he lacked the hypocrisy to deny it, made him feel even more disgusted at himself and his life. He pulled the envelope out of his pocket and reread, in the incomplete summer night, the words that, their bold letters standing out on a white strip of paper, gave the premature appearance of an official death announcement. Laure had fallen under a bus, that very morning, at eleven o'clock. (He wondered what he had been doing at exactly eleven.) Situation critical. He read the service information: the telegram had left that evening and had taken several hours to reach him. No doubt by now it would all be over. The idea that she was no longer in pain lent him a feeling of infinite tenderness, as if all the pain in the world had suddenly ceased to exist. The telegram had been signed by a friend who lived with Laure and whose presence he used to tolerate impatiently; he and that woman had always detested each other, perhaps be-

cause she sincerely loved Laure. For a second, it was
her he was sorry for. Then he wondered how she had
obtained his address. He imagined that sending this
telegram must have brought her the only possible
consolation in her sorrow: the certainty of making
him suffer. To relieve the irritation he called his con-
science, he tried to persuade himself that the unfortunate event was due to nothing but chance, in which
he had no hand; but something dark, deep inside him,
understood that this conjecture withdrew from his
dead mistress the sole beauty left to her, and that the
only nobility of spirit of this woman, who had let herself live, was to have willed her own death.

He lit a match, ignited a corner of the paper, and
watched it burn. A puff of white smoke rose, then disappeared, giving him the feeling of a cremation. He
realized that, for him, Laure had just lost the imper-
fection of existing, had become imponderable, one
with that part of his life which would never return.
With time, she would take her place among those
memories that lend a certain distinction when one

affords oneself the luxury of having had a past. At the same time, he resented her cutting off, with her death, the only road that might have led him back to what he had once been.

Once again he had the melancholy impression that everything works out—which amounts to saying that nothing is ever achieved.

He stepped back into the room, carefully closed the window on the night, and drew the curtains, with a rare sense of docility toward life, conquered or defeated, he too, by the security of closed rooms.

He didn't tell himself, or didn't want to, that this girl from Montparnasse, who was not very bright and had never had much soul, might have found the only possible way out.

AN
EVIL
SPELL

A N ALARM CLOCK showed eleven o'clock, eleven at night. The kitchen was almost spacious; the whitewashed walls, impregnated by cooking vapors, revealed the rings, stains, scratches that are the common signs of use, and next to the door were regular notches by which, year after year, the children had measured their growth. The utensils had been tidied away without symmetry but with a sense of order: the ones used most frequently at easy reach on the lower shelf, and those no longer in use or merely decorative banished to the top. When Ognissanti, newly widowed, had moved into these rooms, they were still lit by oil lamps; now an electric bulb hung from the ceiling, along with a sheet of flypaper. The bulb, the gas stove, the oilcloth spread over the table, a coffee mill bought at the general store in the suburbs, effectively dated the scene and gave it an ageless nobility. Ognissanti, sitting at the table, was talking to a woman who had arrived before the others; they had been putting away the previous night's crockery, and the banality of their movements lent their conversation something uncanny, something weird, by making it part of this commonplace reality.

Several women entered, neighbors. Those over forty looked old; some were thin, already hunched, others fat, bulging out of their shapeless clothes. A tired-looking young woman had brought a child along, unable to leave it on its own. Each new arrival was accompanied by that almost ceremonial exchange of words, insignificant but indispensable, which differ in every social circle but demonstrate all over the world the same attempt at politeness or hospitality. When the neighbors had sat down, Ognissanti offered them coffee; they refused, saying it was best to wait. Someone asked:

"Has she arrived?"

"No," said Ognissanti.

Two young women came in, Ognissanti's daughters. Their presence established the modernity of the scene: their hair was cut short and they were wearing lipstick. The youngest, a linen maid, having worked for several seasons at a large hotel in Nice, had picked up some French slang from the elevator boy and the floor attendants; sometimes misused, it had embedded itself in her Italian dialect.

Then a female step, lighter than the others, echoed softly along the corridor. Ognissanti raised her head:

"Maybe it's her."

But it was only Algenare Nerci, a young neighbor. She was the daughter of refugees from the Piemonte: her father, a communist, had been killed in a scuffle. Shortly after their arrival in France, her mother had died; her brother, who had worked in the marble quarries, had gone off to seek his fortune in Paris; she had stayed on alone. She had earned her living as a maid, then as a seamstress. She was beautiful, with a hard, dark beauty that no one noticed because it was so common among these people and at her age. She sat down on the window seat, next to two other young women. The terrible November *mistral* made the poorly fastened shutters creak; a gust of wind blew into the room; with one hand, Algenare pulled the shutter toward her and leaned her head against it. She closed her eyes. The savage wind reminded her of vague, long-past things she seldom thought of: her childhood home in a mountain village, a grandmother at the spinning wheel, the excitement aroused in her by tales of witchcraft.

Some time later a young man came in. On his face could be seen the battling emotions of sorrow, weariness, and the satisfaction of being considered handsome by the women. He could have been twenty-five. He sat down close to the table. Ognissanti hurriedly made room for him. He asked:

"Is she here?"

It was the second time the question had been asked. Ognissanti shook her head. He continued:

"I'd better fetch her."

"She'll come on her own," Ognissanti said.

He said no more. He too refused coffee. One of Ognissanti's daughters, leaning out of the window, stood up and said:

"There she is."

Only then did he acknowledge the young women's presence. He greeted them clumsily. Everyone noticed that Algenare had grown pale.

At last, the one they were all waiting for arrived. She was wearing a hat in the latest fashion, a fur-lined coat, sheer stockings, and light shoes. Fever and makeup colored her face doubly. Because she had climbed the stairs too fast, she was breathing with difficulty. She greeted everyone with a sort of shy arrogance; having received in life a fair number of insults and having suffered from them, she had grown accustomed to attitudes of defiance. Next to the stove was an empty armchair; she sat down in it. To make room for her, the women drew back their chairs noisily; the woman with the child sat back in the far corner of the room. Their gestures suggested that they were jealous of her beauty, sorry for her because she was sick, and fearful of contagion. Umberto pulled his chair over and sat down next to her.

She said:

"Am I late?"

"No," someone answered.

She pulled a powder compact from her purse and powdered her face. The women, especially the younger ones, cast their eyes over her clothes, her suede purse, her tight string of false pearls. They were angry at Umberto for indulging her invalid fantasies, because it was known that the young chauffeur's family was poor and that he didn't help his own folk. He was her lover, but for the sake of propriety he was called her fiancé—Amanda's fiancé. It is true that he would have married her if she could have been cured, or if his family had agreed that he take charge of a dying woman. It was known that Amanda continued to beg him to marry her as if it were still worthwhile, and she was criticized for wishing to impose useless formalities on the boy, since she was going to die in any case.

He took her hand. He made an effort to show her an even greater tenderness since he had long stopped loving her. After taking her numerous times to the doctors, visiting her in the hospital, buying expensive medications for her, he had forgotten the days when they danced together at the public dance halls outside the city, to which he would drive her, far from other people's gaze, in his master's car, the headlights switched off as they sped down the mountain roads, the sensations of their two bodies mingling with the illusion of a vicarious luxury. He had stopped making love to her since death had visibly possessed her: Amanda had become for him a sort of sad devotion. This affection, which was no longer love since it lacked the means love has of satisfying itself, could only express itself in symbols, like devotion to God. Being with the sick woman taught the simple young man the refinements of suffering: Umberto, sitting at Amanda's feet, held the hand that was too hot and whose touch was now painful to him, and all kinds of obscure, almost mystical feelings of duty, pity, and fear made up his fidelity.

She said:

"I'm cold, Aunt."

Ognissanti, remembering that she hadn't offered her anything, suggested coffee, rum. She drank, then ate, revealing her gums as she did so. At times she even loved her illness, without which, married or not, Umberto would have left her for other women—an illness which, like all dying people, she didn't think would kill her. She had never had another lover, so she only had Umberto to blame for what she called her misfortune; he was the only being who had ever afforded her the pleasure of blaming someone for something. Since everything that had happened, according to her, was his fault, she felt she had the right to ask for the impossible; her demands served both as revenge and as proof to herself and others that a man could still devote himself to her entirely. Jealous of every woman, she still thought herself superior to all others, since now they all strove to be of service to her, and their reluctance to touch her, to kiss her, made her proud of her ability to make someone afraid. Not one of these women didn't hate her, for the very reason that pity forced them to love her; they begrudged her the care they thought they had to give her, just as a debtor begrudges his creditors his own

integrity. Amanda's malice irritated even those who
would weep at her deathbed; all day long they were
annoyed by her difficult, insolent, insatiable manners,
and failed to understand that a sinister smile, a small
treachery, an insult, in Amanda's case were as certainly the result of her sickness and its debilitating
symptoms as were her loss of weight, her cough, the
failing of her voice.

Someone asked:

"And your child?"

She told them all that he now weighed twenty
pounds. The vigor of the small being who had lived
inside her, lived off her, but whom she had been forbidden to breast-feed and would soon be forbidden to
kiss, was revenge for her, almost compensation. Detached by the distance not only from her body but
also from her heart, he was growing up somewhere
in the country, in the care of a woman employed to
raise him, and Amanda rarely thought of him, ab-
sorbed as she increasingly was by the inner labors of
her sickness, as in a mortal pregnancy. Since she

hardly knew her child, she felt pride in him rather than love for him, and sometimes she hated him, as if by coming into this world he had robbed her of her life.

Ognissanti said:

"Twenty minutes to midnight."

It was the time at which Cattaneo d'Aigues was expected, the man who, in that region, was known as a clever healer, someone capable of breaking spells. Seeing Amanda fade away in spite of the potions and the injections, her neighbors, sisters, and aunt had finally asked him to come. All the women believed that Amanda was under an evil spell, cast either by a rival or by a witch incapable of not doing harm, even for no profit, just as certain beasts are incapable of not spewing out poison. Everything had been tried, even a pilgrimage to Lourdes, even a trip to Marseilles to consult famous professors. Faced with the failure of both faith and science, both of which seemed to accept and even approve the certainty of death, these people turned toward more ancient and, according to them, more proven practices: the magician who treats death as an invisible adversary, tries to frighten it away, and fights it face to face. Despairing of doctors, Umberto agreed to the ordeal. The women had started suspecting one another, and many of them may have turned up at this event the better to prove their own innocence.

"We can begin," said Ognissanti.

"We could have done this at my place, Aunt," said Amanda.

The idea of undressing in front of all these women, in that unfamiliar room, filled her with unexpected fear and modesty.

"Your place is too small," said Ognissanti.

A woman who occupied the room next door offered it to Amanda so that she might undress at her ease. Both women went out. At the door they met Cattaneo d'Aigues. Amanda squeezed herself against the wall; he said to her:

"Is it you, my dear?"

She didn't answer; he went in. The women admired him for recognizing the sick woman without anyone's having to point her out, as if Amanda's appearance were not advertisement enough. He apologized for being late, complained about the weather, undid his coat, sat down in the armchair Amanda had vacated. He spoke little. He was an insignificant man who worked as an accountant during the day; to these nightmarish settings he brought a bureaucratic formality. He walked over to the stove and noticed with cool anger that they had almost let the fire die out. Algenare rose to feed it. Because she was the poorest, they treated her as a servant.

The women huddled together. One said:

"And if no one has wished her evil, what will we see in the water?"

"Nothing," the man said.

Ognissanti insisted:

"If no one had wished her evil, she wouldn't be where she is now."

She felt obliged, because of family ties, to testify to the health of her kin.

"All the same, her mother and father both died of the same illness," Umberto said.

He enjoyed reminding them of this as he himself felt that his own health was tenuous and feared that someone might accuse him of having infected her with the disease.

"This illness isn't natural," said Ognissanti.

She didn't think she had said the right thing. For these men and women there was no such thing as a natural illness; perhaps nothing was ever natural. Their universe was still in chaos, and all occurrences, even the simplest, remained mysteries for them, though some events, being more frequent than others, became customary to them. The phases of the moon, the making of fire in their kitchen stoves, were no less inconceivable for them than the burrowing of caverns in sick lungs; in their eyes, only the death of the old was natural, that is to say, fair. And yet, since they were human beings, condemned by the instinct of their species to seek and perhaps invent causes, they attributed Amanda's languishing to the cause that for them was the simplest, the most human of all, the force whose effects they had so often witnessed throughout their lives: envy, one woman's jealousy of another.

Someone said faintly:

"It's true, it must have worn her out, raising her brothers and sisters all by herself."

There was a silence. No one, certainly not Amanda's aunt, wanted to think how hard it had been for this stubborn young girl, herself no more than a child, to feed her young siblings. The mention of work, of Amanda's courage, wounded them all, as if they were all suspected of being somehow inferior in her regard, inferior in suffering or in fatigue.

"Well!" Ognissanti exclaimed, "as if we hadn't all worked as hard as her!"

In Umberto's presence, a certain modesty stopped them from mentioning the other causes of her sickness: the strikers' meetings on damp nights, the humid heat of the dance halls, the succession of difficult births. Amanda returned, her coat wrapped tightly around her; her pale legs imitated the copper color of her stockings, and as she was used to wearing high-heeled shoes, she was walking on tiptoe.

Cattaneo said:

"Where are your things?"

She was carrying them under her arm. She put them on a chair, methodically rolled them into a bundle, the shoes in the middle with the stockings wrapped around them, then the slip around both, and finally the dress. It was a dress made of delicate, light-colored silk. Vanity had prevented her from choosing the older one, and now she regretted the sacrifice.

Algenare went over to help her. Roughly, Ognissanti said:

"No."

Algenare drew back. Amanda looked up, not understanding. They were friends. At the beginning of her relationship with Umberto, Algenare had often lent them her room. She was grateful for it, never imagining that the solitary woman, who had the reputation of being chaste, sought her pleasure in living and sleeping in an atmosphere where others had made love.

Cattaneo d'Aigues now took a new kettle and dropped in the slender bundle, suggestive of mortal spoils. They sat down again. The water took its time to come to a boil, as it always does when being watched; the women spoke in low voices of diseases, deaths, and mysterious healings, exchanging the same few ideas again and again, in different ways. The scene, played out at several levels, would have disappointed both lovers of the picturesque and lovers of drama; the thoughts, the instincts, sprang up from the depths of ages, but the two men and the women, sitting in a kitchen under an electric light, waiting for the water to boil in a nickel kettle used for dirty linen, would have offered an observer the banal, weekly, almost ritual scene of someone doing the laundry.

Simple people believe that silence during inaction is something unnatural. They habitually associate silence with work, for it allows them to withdraw from themselves (work, on the other hand, may be the de-

votion of the poor), and they confuse repose with the
act of telling stories. And yet here they all kept quiet out
of respect for their own waiting; their hands, as inac-
tive as their lips, rested on their knees, fingers spread,
with awkward tranquillity, and this halt in the flow of
life, this deferential passivity, reminded them of that
other half-hour of combined repose and constraint,
which is the Sunday High Mass. The water began to
sing; the women found something disturbing in the
sound, something solemn, bearing no relation to the
daily filtering of coffee and the sift of the egg timer.
Amanda, wrapped in her coat, trembled not with cold
but with impatience, with fear; she had heard it said
that those on whom a spell is cast will die if the one who
cast the spell is sought out. Her sickness, being within
her, did not seem external or foreign to her, something
that could be taken away or given to someone else; it
had now become confusingly linked to the idea she had
of herself, like a presence that little by little was taking
her place. Algenare, sitting on the other side of the
room, was silent; Cattaneo d'Aigues had his eye on the

alarm clock. When both hands met at the top of the clock's face, he rose, took the kettle off the fire, placed it on a chair, and said to Amanda:

"Come."

Meekly she drew near. The steam blinded her; she bent over; she was trying, without success, to distinguish an outline in the shapeless boiling mass in which, here and there, a piece of clothing swelled up. She would have liked to see something, if only to calm her anguish, not to have waited in vain, naked under her coat, among those women chattering about black magic; if only not to disappoint the others by betraying their vigil. Since everyone else, in a similar situation, was bound to see something, why should she not make anything out? She tried to remember the faces of rivals, enemies; she tried to invent them, to project them outside herself. The bubbling water didn't even return her own image. She faltered. The women tried to come closer. Cattaneo d'Aigues kept them away with a single gesture. Placing his hand on her fragile shoulder, he said:

"Look closely. The woman who wished you evil will appear to you in the water. Her hair . . . "

He passed his hand over Amanda's hair, like a mesmerizer. She repeated, with desperately empty eyes:

"Her hair . . . "

He continued, creating the image piece by piece:

"Her eyes . . . "

"Her eyes . . . "

"Her mouth . . . "

"Her mouth . . . "

Algenare had fallen to her knees.

"Don't look anymore, Amanda! Don't look! You won't see anything. It's not me. You won't see anything."

She was stammering. Dragging herself along the floor, she repeated:

"It isn't me, is it? It isn't me?"

Amanda raised her hands to her face and said:

"I've always known it."

And she fell back into her chair. She was overcome by a fit of coughing. Her lips were stained with blood, and she opened her purse and pulled out her handkerchief.

This time the women rose and made a circle around the young unfortunate who had accused herself by her denials. Cattaneo d'Aigues seemed not to hear. He opened the drawer of a kitchen cabinet, chose a knife, tested the tip, and handed it to Amanda.

She looked at it stupidly, without understanding. Then he said to her:

"You're to plunge the knife into the water at the spot where you saw the image. You're to stab to the hilt, even if the water resists, even if it cries out . . . "

He added after a moment's thought:

"Even if it bleeds."

"Will I get better?"

"Yes," the man said.

Amanda stood up. She continued:

"And she will die?"

One could hardly hear her.

"Yes," the man said.

Algenare howled rather than cried:

"I don't want to be killed."

Amanda, leaning over the kettle, looked into the water. The water that was about to cry out, resist, bleed, terrified her as much as if it were a woman of flesh and blood, even more than a woman of flesh and blood. She was angry at Cattaneo d'Aigues, who by warning her had prevented her from acting. One acts without knowing what will take place, in order to know. She had often told herself that she'd kill Umberto if he ever left her. But he was not going to leave her. No one was leaving her. She couldn't hate that woman for wishing her death; in her place she would have done the same. She couldn't hate her because that woman wasn't loved. Umberto didn't love her. She felt like laughing out loud: what kind of woman was this, what kind of witch was this who wasn't even capable of making someone love her? She tried to imagine the suffering Algenare might have caused her, the casting of further spells, the evil eye. She was unable to. Among the women who pitied her, who

believed that in pitying her they were freeing themselves from her, there was one who envied her, envied
her enough to wish her dead. Her happiness stood in
someone's way, and she felt happy. Triumphantly, she
watched the woman writhing on the floor.

The inciting murmur of the water filled her ears,
mingling with the beating of her arteries; she would
not have guessed that her body still contained that
much blood. Memories flooded back to her from the
depths of her childhood, as if from a faraway country
to which she would never return; clear, cutting images that had become almost absurd since they were
no longer related to anything: a rabbit to be slaugh-
tered in the kitchen for Sunday dinner; her mother
crying out to her to hurry; she didn't have the courage
to cut into the fur: it was alive, it fought back, it
poured its life out in a manner she had not foreseen,
it was awful. Then, one day, still a child, she had been
placed as a servant with a woman who gave her little
to eat, wore her out, beat her. She hadn't wanted to
be a servant any longer: she had tried to cut off her

thumb so as not to be made to work any longer. The blood flowed, it couldn't be stopped. She put her thumb in her mouth and sucked it; her mouth was full of blood. She swallowed it, with difficulty. She asked herself: If the water in the kettle were now to fill up with blood, would anything be left clean, clear, drinkable in the whole world? Out loud, she said:

"I'm so thirsty!"

No one heard her. She was choking; the knife slid from her hands. Seeing her falter, the women rushed forward.

Cattaneo d'Aigues slipped on his coat. He was not a tender man. Amanda's death, now certain to come, seemed to him an event somehow legitimized by everyone's certainty of it—painful for those close to her; cruel for her lover, at least during the first few hours; profitable perhaps for the child rescued from a useless mother, a mother he would not miss since he had never known her; but in any case indifferent to Cattaneo. He was disappointed. Warning Amanda that the water might bleed, he had simply followed the usual wording; in spite of having often presided over this ritual and believing in its efficacy, he had never seen any blood. At most, the woman on whom a spell had been cast had perceived a resistance, heard a cry. He didn't doubt that the complete phenomenon had not been allowed to take place, and, like a scientist determined to have another try at an experiment that has never worked, he relentlessly persisted in producing a miracle, going from sick person to sick person. He was angry at Amanda for not having backed him up, under particularly favorable circumstances since for once the spell-caster had been present. This clever peasant, only interested in facts, brought to his magic formulas the soul of a materialist practitioner, just as certain men of science, at their patients' bedside, display the soul of a miracle worker.

He crossed the room; he fixed his eyes on Algenare; she had remained collapsed on the red tiles of the floor, not weeping, but with the sound of sobbing in her throat. He said to her:

"So you are the one who hurt her?"

Now he was no longer curious about anything except her. She remained silent; he listed the various methods for casting spells: piercing the heart of a bull, burying a lemon under the threshold, burning fingernail clippings. At each phrase she shook her head wildly; in the end, she said:

"No . . . No . . . I wished it . . . Just wished it . . . "

He felt a sudden respect for her, almost admiration, as if for an adversary whose might one has just discovered.

"Ah," he said. "Then you're very powerful . . . "

He left. Vague images crossed Algenare's mind; she remembered the arrival of the fascists at her father's house. She had been beaten; she had waited, sitting on the floor, hunched over, for the tempest of men to pass. She wondered what these women were waiting for: Why weren't they beating her, chasing her away? Would Umberto kill her now? She raised her head. Umberto was weeping in a corner. Almost with impatience, she waited for the insults to begin:

the air was dense, vibrant, pregnant with cries and words that were not addressed to her. Since the turmoil did not concern her, it was the same as silence.

She stood up to her full height. The women were busy around Amanda, who had fainted. Her coat had slid off her shoulders; her naked body, thin, white, smooth as a kernel no longer hidden by shell and pulp, seemed simultaneously to contain and to expose death as if in a display case. Her head lay against the back of the chair; Algenare couldn't see her face. A certain curiosity prompted her, perhaps the dim hope of something irredeemable. Leaning forward, she mechanically put her hand on the shoulder of one of the women, who turned round with a cry. It was the child's mother. The woman drew back, saying humbly:

"My son hasn't done anything to you yet."

And she tried to cover the child's small face with her handkerchief. Then, for the first time, Algenare understood that something had changed, that she now terrified these women. She felt neither astonishment nor triumph: these people had entered, that evening, one of those cycles in which the extraordinary begets the extraordinary, logically, as in the geometry of nightmares. She said to herself, with physical relief, that she would not be beaten, that she would be allowed to leave, that they wanted her to leave. The whistling of the wind through the blinds reminded her that she would be cold outside; she glanced around the room for something. Out loud she said:

"My shawl . . . "

The women's eyes swept the room. The fringe of the shawl was dangling on the ground; on her way in, she had hung it on the back of the chair on which Amanda was now sitting. Someone lifted Amanda's head, which was lolling from side to side with childish unconsciousness. Umberto pulled at the shawl, but it resisted, no doubt held back by some invisible asperity; and the slowness with which he had to proceed gave that simple act an unexpected, almost unbearable importance, which would not have been noticed had it lasted a shorter time. Umberto folded the square piece of material, methodically, as if it were worth the effort, and handed it over to Algenare. Their eyes met; in Umberto's there was no anger, not even surprise, nothing but the emptiness into which we are cast by submission or misfortune.

Only then did the remainder of her amorous hopes vanish, hopes strong because, unaware of them, she hadn't even been able to call them absurd; she realized she would never belong to this man, nor ever, indeed, to any other. Fear, along with possibilities of hatred, quenched all possibilities of love. Now that a test that they all deemed decisive had revealed in her the mysterious power of doing evil, these people would no longer be shocked at the wrongs they supposed she had done, or at those she might do. All of them silently remembered symptoms they had long neglected, or that had troubled them without actually causing them concern: her quiet assurance in the presence of wild animals, strange noises that could be heard when she was there, glimmers in her eyes. They also remembered that a child left in her care had suffered sudden death. A certain pity, sprung from the ancient memory of persecutions and bonfires, renewed in their more recent experience by the sight of witches suffering from fits of hysteria, mingling with their fear of her, turned almost to a terrified form of respect. An obscure sense of the world's economy led them to admit the existence of beings different from others, beings whose behavior scandalizes reason, and sometimes the heart. Their act of faith or resignation toward their Creator asserted even the need for witches. Expressing this rather confused notion by a symbol that was not without beauty, these Catholic peasants believed the sacrifice of Mass could not be accomplished without a servant of the old enemy, the old accuser (but who was also, after all, God's old helpmate) roaming in the church's vicinity. And naturally lending the clergy an organizing role in the spiritual world, which is the background and the matrix of the other, they supposed that the priest, on certain days of the year, marked the child being brought to baptism with a sign that would predestine it to the painful but indispensable task of becoming a little servant of evil.

Algenare wrapped herself in the shawl, shivering, as if the cold of the street had already reached her. No one said a word: Amanda was gasping and wheezing, her breathing increasingly spasmodic, and these sounds—the animal effort perceptible beneath her naked breasts, the quivers, the symptoms of an inner upheaval—were like the mechanical face of death itself. When she had finished pinning on her shawl, Algenare moved to the door: they all watched in silence as it closed behind her.

She walked down the unlighted steps as cautiously as a blind woman. Below, the stub of a candle was burning in a corner; a cat, recognizing her, came and rubbed itself against her legs, expecting to be stroked. She bent down; for a moment, the innocence of the cat responded to her own dark innocence. Not for a second did she doubt that she had killed Amanda by wishing for her death; she didn't doubt it because no one doubted it. At the same time, the certainty of

a strange power effaced the remorse caused by any
ordinary crime, offering her a sense of irresponsibil-
ity that was not an excuse but a justification. Someone
possessing such power would lose any reason to live,
unless as the power's instrument. Having never heard
that witches felt shame, she began to fulfill her role
and felt shame no longer. Even though Amanda had
been dear to her, even though she had loved Amanda
the more because she had envied her, having somehow merged with her after taking Amanda's place
so many times in her own imagination, Algenare
abruptly stopped feeling sorry for her, because someone who casts spells doesn't feel sorry for her victims.
The certain knowledge that Umberto would feel
nothing but horror for her—the more so since it
might allow him to hide from himself the secret relief
this death would bring—this knowledge, the only
one she was able to grasp, precise, weighing heavily
on her like a foreign body, deprived Algenare of the
benefit of her desire to kill, which she mistook for an
actual deed. Forgetting that this obsession sprang

from the simplest of instincts, certainly the most un-
derstandable, she thought of it now as merely gratu-
itous because the event itself had proved it useless.
Not to profit from it removed not only the remorse of
having caused it but also the very notion of having
had a hidden interest in that death, as if the act, having been without profit, thus acquired the mysterious,
almost ennobling aura of having been without cause.

Some women who had come downstairs behind
her pressed themselves against the wall so as not to
brush past her on the threshold; she heard them mut-
ter that Amanda would not live past dawn. Then the
faint specters overtook her and vanished into the
dark. It was now raining. Algenare, wrapping her
shawl even more tightly around her, headed down the
narrow cobbled street. As she walked, she thought.

She didn't reflect. She was one of those women
who never reflect but instead think in a succession of
images: the lowered blind of a cleaner's shop reminded her that Ognissanti had asked her to come
next day to help with the washing; she wouldn't have

to go, they would no longer expect her. She told herself, with sudden joy, that she would no longer have to offer small neighborly services, grind the evening coffee, light the morning fire. Nor would there be any more idle talks with young men under the streetlights, village dances under the red glow of the lanterns, workshop outings in the spring. She was alone. The power they attributed to her, and which henceforth she attributed to herself, was like those ancient sorcerers' circles that both isolate and protect. Like the king in the legend who turned everything in his presence into gold, from now on everything around her would be turned into terror. At the same time, she was no longer alone. She felt attached, through space, by links that were strong because invisible, to the community of those who are persecuted, flattered, revered, all at the same time; to the scattered fraternity of spell-casters, secret folk, village sorcerers. This young woman who until then had gained nothing either from life or from herself experienced the intimate, organic exultation of those who have just discovered love or have a presentiment of fame: something unknown, which was transforming her, was being born within her. A ready-made personality, infinitely richer than her own, was replacing hers, a personality to which she would try to conform to the day of her death.

She stopped by a puddle left by the last downpour, bent over in the glow of a lighted window, caught sight of her own face, and burst out laughing. She laughed, with a laugh she herself had not expected, wild, of a wickedness that persuaded her she had been transformed or, rather, had found herself. Not only her heart but the face of the world had changed for her: a forgotten broom in a courtyard, a pin in her corsage, the bleating of a goat through the stable wall reminded her no longer of the common, easy acts of ordinary life, but of spells and witches' sabbaths, and as she threw back her head the better to breathe in the night air, the stars drew for her, in large trembling strokes, the giant letters of the witches' alphabet.